Make a Wish,
Henry Bear

Liam Francis Walsh

A NEAL PORT
ROARING BRO
NEW YO

To Alessia, my wish come true

t was the night before Henry Bear's birthday. He pulled the covers up to his nose and reached over to switch off the light.

"Can't you stay up a little bit longer?" asked Mama Bear.

"Just ten more minutes?" begged Papa Bear. "Pleeeeease?"

Henry got out of bed with a sigh. "Fine," he said. "Ten more minutes, but that's *all*."

They went into the backyard
to climb trees.

"Higher!" called Mama Bear.
"Go, Henry, go!"

"It's okay!" called Papa Bear.
"Don't be scared!"

There was
a loud *crack*.

"Ouch!" said Henry.
"That was fun!" said Mama Bear.
"Let's go play on the swing!" said Papa
Bear. "I'll push you really, *really* high!"

"It's late," said Henry, "and tomorrow is
a school day."
"Let's go ride bikes!" said Mama Bear.
"Good idea!" said Papa Bear.
"Good night!" said Henry.

The next morning, Henry was so tired he could hardly get out of bed. When he finally dragged himself to breakfast, this is what he saw:

"Not *again*," groaned Henry.

"But it's your birthday, dear," said Mama Bear.

"Yes," said Henry, "but we had chocolate cake for dinner!"

"And for lunch and breakfast, too!" said Papa Bear, smacking his lips.

"I'm not hungry," said Henry. "I'll just wait in the car."

"I have an idea," said Papa Bear. "Why don't we all stay home and watch TV!"

"But I have to go to school!" said Henry.

"That sounds boring," said Mama Bear. "You'd better take some toys."

So Henry
hurried
off to
school.

"Oh dear," he thought. "I hope I won't be late again."

"You're late again, Henry!" said Mr. Bindle.

"I'm sorry," said Henry.

"Did you do your homework?" asked Mr. Bindle.

"I didn't have time," said Henry. "I had to help my parents draw on the walls."

"Again?" said Mr. Bindle.

At midday, Henry was frowning into his lunchbox when he heard a voice ask, "May I sit here?"

It was a girl he'd never seen before, but Henry knew you should always be extra friendly to new students, so he said, "Of course."

The girl's name was Marjani.

"I've never seen someone with a slice of chocolate cake looking so unhappy," said Marjani.

So Henry told her the whole story.

"On my last birthday, when I blew out the candles, I wished my mom and dad were more fun," said Henry. "Now, for a whole year they've been feeding me cake and getting me into trouble. So tonight, when I blow out my candles, I'm going to wish them back to the way they were."

"Wow," said Marjani. "Oh, and happy birthday," she added.

That gave Henry an idea. "Would you like to come over after school?" he asked. "For my birthday?"

"I'd like that very much," said Marjani.

When Henry got home from school, he went to tell Mama Bear about his new friend. He found her in the kitchen with an enormous bowl of candy.

"Aren't we having birthday cake?" asked Henry.

"We always have cake," said Mama Bear, "so tonight we're having candy instead."

"Oh no!" said Henry. "What about birthday candles?"

"Silly," said Mama Bear. "You can't put candles on candies, can you?"

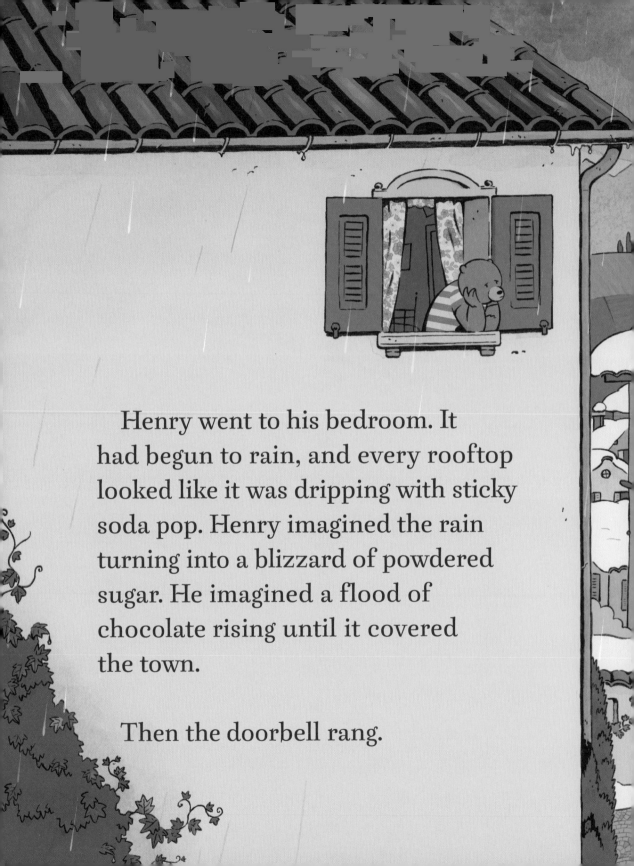

Henry went to his bedroom. It had begun to rain, and every rooftop looked like it was dripping with sticky soda pop. Henry imagined the rain turning into a blizzard of powdered sugar. He imagined a flood of chocolate rising until it covered the town.

Then the doorbell rang.

Mama Bear, Papa Bear, Henry, and
Marjani sat down at the table.

"Do you like to rock on your chair?"
Papa Bear asked Marjani. "I do."

"Me too!" said Mama Bear.

They sang "Happy Birthday" to Henry.

"Make a wish!" whispered Marjani.

Later, after Marjani had gone home, Mama and Papa Bear were tucking Henry into bed.

"Today was so much fun," said Henry. "Can I stay up for just ten more minutes? Pleeeeease?"

"You need your sleep, Henry. Tomorrow is a school day," said Mama Bear. "Good night."

"Sleep tight, Henry," said Papa Bear.

And Henry did.